eye 2 i  i 2 eye

the written word
meets the visual

Rugby Writers
Rugby Artists' Group

I0713192

Published in parallel to the exhibition:
  eye 2 i, i 2 eye
  Rugby Art Gallery and Museum, Rugby, UK
  14th January – 17th March 2012

Rugby Art Gallery and Museum
Little Elborow Street
Rugby, Warwickshire
CV21 3BZ
www.ragm.org.uk

ISBN 978-1-4709-7978-2

© 2012 Rugby Writers. Rugby Artists' Group.

First edition 2012
All rights reserved. No part of this publication may be
reproduced, stored in a retrieval system, or transmitted,
in any forms or by any means, without prior permission
in writing of the authors, nor be otherwise circulated in
any form of binding or cover other than that in which it
is published and without similar condition including this
condition being imposed on the subsequent purchaser.

FOREWORD

Every year Rugby Art Gallery and Museum support exhibition projects created by artists based in the borough of Rugby. Artists apply to the art gallery by submitting an exhibition proposal which is considered by a selection panel made up of Rugby Borough Councillors. The panel aims to select an exhibition that will contain high quality, vibrant art works and will also compliment the programme of exhibitions and education events at the gallery. This year the panel selected a highly creative proposal submitted jointly by Rugby Artists' Group and Rugby Writers: *eye 2 i, i 2 eye.*

The *eye 2 i, i 2 eye* project was set up as a collaboration between Rugby Writers and Rugby Artists' Group. The premise of the collaboration involved writers and visual artists loaning work to each other in order to inspire new pieces of work to be made. Each artist loaned an art work to a writer and each writer loaned a piece of writing to an artist. The resulting exhibition contains all of the original work alongside the new pieces created in response, and this book serves as a permanent record of all sixty-eight items. The exhibition is an intriguing mix of writing and art works in a variety of styles and mediums highlighting the wealth of cultural endeavour which takes place within the borough of Rugby.

Jess Morgan
Senior Exhibitions Officer
Rugby Art Gallery and Museum

ACKNOWLEDGEMENTS

The *eye 2 i, i 2 eye* Steering Group were Glyn Essex (RW), Laurence Tilley (RAG), Augustus Stephens (RW) and Marion Reid (RAG). We should like to warmly express our thanks to Eric Gaskell for his untiring work in the design and setting of this book; to Bernard Daniels for serving as project photographer; to Jessica Morgan, Monica Fernandez, and all the staff at Rugby Museum and Art Gallery for their encouragement during the project process and work in enabling the exhibition; to Emily Tilley who gave us the project title; to our families and friends for their patience and to all the *eye 2 i, i 2 eye* participants, for their creativity, encouragement, enthusiasm and fellowship.

INTRODUCTIONS

This project has probably provoked more discussion among Rugby Writers than anything else we've done. Writing about a picture, photograph or other piece of visual art has long been a staple of creative writing exercises so at one level it was not new to us. Having an original piece of art in our care for a good length of time, however, and being able to discuss it with the artist who would see the outcome of our take on it added to the challenge facing us.

I think most of us rapidly moved away from the idea of interpreting the piece or making any sort of direct commentary on it. Instead, we seem to have responded at a deeper level and to have taken off fearlessly into the unknown – rather like a flight with Ryanair but one upgraded by the quality of the art we travelled with.

We hope you enjoy it.

Glyn Essex
Rugby Writers

Art is a dance, a juggle, a battle of mind and heart. Without intelligence, technique and wisdom, quality art is rarely produced, and without passion even technically proficient art will bore the viewer. The task of responding visually to the written down thoughts of another human being challenges the artist first to decide whether to illustrate directly or to branch off on a reciprocal flight of new imagining. In *eye 2 i, i 2 eye* artists were free to take either path. They were urged not to feel obliged to please their writer, but to be unconstrained and make from their own thoughts, arising from what they read, works which would primarily please themselves - Art from the heart, in the hope that it would also please others. We hope that some of it pleases you.

Laurence G. Tilley
Rugby Artists' Group

CONTENTS

In the gallery *by Wendy Goulstone* 8
   In the gallery *by Dawn Russell (Oil) a response to "In the Gallery"*
Robin *by Dawn Russell (Oil)* 10
   Robin *by Wendy Goulstone a response to "Robin"*
———————

Revelation *by Rupert Smith* 12
   Post Revelation – Let's Talk *by Susan K Haynes (Felt) a response to "Revelation"*
Morning Cuppa *by Susan K Haynes (Acrylic)* 14
   All is Image *by Rupert Smith a response to "Morning Cuppa"*
———————

Mama's Box *by Kathy Newitt* 16
   Remembrance (2011) *by Ann Power (Sand blasted mirror surface) a response to "Mama's Box"*
Salamanca Series IIIb (2009) *by Ann Power (Watercolour)* 18
   Monica's Cupboard *by Kathy Newitt a response to "Salamnca Series IIIb"*
———————

In the Beginning… *by Gemma Hammond* . . 20
   Suspended *by Lindsay Kyle (Mixed Media) a response to "In the Beginnning"*
Poppies – An explosion in Red *by Lindsay Kyle (Mixed Media)* 22
   Remembrance Days *by Gemma Hammond a response to "Poppies – An Explosion in Red"*

Enigma *by Marcia Phillpott* 24
   Churchyard in Moonlight *by Anna Phillips (Pencil) a response to "Enigma"*
Cement Works in Moonlight *by Anna Phillips (Drypoint)* 26
   Triptych *by Marcia Phillpott a response to "Cement Works in Moonlight"*
———————

Coromandel *by William S Chapman* 28
   Transient Memories *by Sheila Lucas (Watercolour) a response to "Coromandel"*
Work to do *by Sheila Lucas (Watercolour)* . . . 30
   See This Room *by William S Chapman a response to "Work to do"*
———————

The Horned One *by Augustus Stephens* . . . 32
   The Horned One *by Marion Reid (Oil) a response to "The Horned One"*
Sweet Smell of Destruction *by Marion Reid (Acrylic)* 34
   Demon in a Bottle *by Augustus Stephens a response to "Sweet Smell of Destruction"*
———————

Two Faced *by Hazel Bowden* 36
   Smile Please! *by Joan Green (Woodcut) a response to "Two Faced"*
Raku Fired Form *by Joan Green (Ceramic)* . 38
   My Raku *by Hazel Bowden a response to "Raku Fired Form"*
———————

opera tickets (bluster in a hurricane) *by Scott Baker* 40
   Dark Moods *by Winifred Wilmot (Acrylic) a response to "opera tickets"*
Flash *by Winifred Wilmot (Oil)* 42
   flash *by Scott Baker a response to "Flash"*

Clouds *by Glyn Essex* 44
  Cloud Gazer *by Laurence G Tilley (Ceramic)*
  a response to "Clouds"

Exile Cup *by Laurence G Tilley (Ceramic).* . . . 46
  Diaspora *by Glyn Essex a response to "Exile*
  Cup"

—————

Fossil History *by Nicholas Marsh* 48
  The Rain-stop Diptych *by Carol Wheeler*
  (Mixed Media) a response to "Fossil History"

Hungarian Fantasy *by Carol Wheeler (Mixed*
Media) 50
  Return to the Fishermen's Bastion *by*
  Nicholas Marsh a response to "Hungarian
  Fantasy"

—————

Damage *by Debbie Hibberd.* 52
  Stage Set IV (Damage) *by Eric Gaskell*
  (Mixed Media) a response to "Damage"

Table in a Room *by Eric Gaskell (Linocut).* . . 54
  Extra Cup *by Debbie Hibberd a response*
  to "Table in a Room"

—————

Great Oaks from Little Acorns Grow
by Lin Jennings 56
  Imagine *by Mo Enright (Oil) a response to*
  "Great Oaks from Little Acorns Grow"

Waiting for Curtain Call *by Mo Enright (Oil)* 58
  I Dreamt Behind Makeshift Curtains
  by Lin Jennings a response to "Waiting for
  Curtain Call"

Sardinian Harvest *by Debs de Vries* 60
  Papaule ruju *by Margarita Rubra (Paper)*
  a response to "Sardinian Harvest"

Hedgerow *by Margarita Rubra (Mixed Media)* 62
  Flotsam *by Debs de Vries a response to*
  "Hedgerow"

—————

A linocut *a draft for J.K.* *by Nigel Sinker* . . 64
  Floribunda *by Vivienne Garrod-Grinnell*
  (Mixed Media) a response to "A Linocut"

Autumnal Joy *by Vivienne Garrod-Grinnell*
(Clay and Glass) 66
  Vivienne's Bowl *by Nigel Sinker a response*
  to "Autumnal Joy"

—————

Abigail *by Marion Clare* 68
  Perception of Memory and Emotion
  by Judy Haslam-Jones (Mixed Media) a
  response to "Abigail"

Three Temple Boxes *by Judy Haslam-Jones*
(Stoneware) 70
  Dom Raja – A Portrait *by Marion Clare*
  a response to "Three Temple Boxes"

—————

Worm Holes *by Stephanie F. Goodacre* 72
  Worm Holes *by Therése Kane (Pencil) a*
  response to "Worm Holes"

Remnants – Auntie Bernadette
by Therése Kane (Pencil) 74
  Song for Edith *by Stephanie F. Goodacre a*
  response to "Remnants – Auntie Bernadette"

In the gallery *by Wendy Goulstone*

Madonna and child, tiger wild,
unmade bed, Baptist's head,
Icarus' fall, death by wall,
Picasso's daughter, infant slaughter,
rain, speed and steam, silent scream,
earring pearl, blind girl,
piano upside down, foreign town,
de Morgan tile, bricks in pile,
light bulbs off and on, battle won,
gigantic spider, triumphant rider,
distant cape, Sabine rape,
seeds on floor, hell and war,
Venus on shell, war and hell.

In the gallery *by Dawn Russell (Oil on Canvas)*
a response to "In the Gallery"

Robin *by Dawn Russell (Oil on canvas)*

Robin *by Wendy Goulstone*
a response to "Robin"

4th March:
Rain stopped at last.
Dug the potato patch.
Turned my back and there he was,
perched on the spade.

21st April:
Glorious day.
Sat with coffee on the terrace.
Down he flew, head cocked,
expecting crumbs.

16th May:
A scorcher.
Angry squawking in the ivy.
Next door's cat on the prowl.
Fingers crossed.

19th October:
A nip in the air.
I held a sultana on my palm.
He hopped over and ate it.
What joy!

27th December:
Bitter wind. Snow forecast.
He pecked Christmas cake
and looked me in the eye.
Ice on the birdbath.

3rd January:
Minus 14

Revelation *by Rupert Smith*

I know you have had a hard time
I trace the wound
the fingertips are still fresh
sorrow shrinks the soul
pain and punishment
the human condition

… a cold wind blows in from the east
the sky is angry
dark
glowering incoherently …
your eyes look like rain
what did you expect?
I shrug my shoulders
I make no excuses
although I regret the collateral
damage
you knew the score

… though the trees are bare they are
beginning to bud
smoke from a distant chimney curls
into a question mark
a hawk hovers high
in the air …

have we had an epiphany?
hatred is a hard taskmaster
soon you will understand

Post Revelation – Let's Talk *by Susan K Haynes (Felted wool fibres)*
a response to "Revelation"

Morning Cuppa *by Susan K Haynes (Acrylic on Canvas)*

All is Image *by Rupert Smith*
a response to "Morning Cuppa"

All Is Image
Consider the light; its brightness,
Celerity, the depth
Of its information. For us the light
Defines reality and
Gives it context. But what we see
Is merely an aspect
Of reality, a facet, a shadow, an
Image and it is this
That is the artist's raw material.
Whether painter,
Writer or poet we must strive to
Make the image
Fresh, imbue it with new meaning.
Here the artist
Has captured the image of a kettle
On canvas, reflected
From its shiny surface is a secondary
Image of a man and
A woman who are seated on folding
Chairs, drinking
Mugs of tea. Who are these people?
What are their
Origins? Are they lovers, friends,
Conspirators or what?
Perhaps they are all three and are
Sworn to silence.
I like to think of them as the artist
And her spouse whom
She has kettled in an infinite future
Of companionable solitude.

Mama's Box *by Kathy Newitt*

I remove the tiny clothes from the old box, an outfit my mother knit for my baby doll many years ago.

My mind wanders to the time Mr Herbert shared with me a piece of his distant past.

When I presented him with a gift I'd parcelled up in this old box that day, he appeared distracted. It was only some cakes I'd baked and the cigar box, lined with waxed paper, had proved a handy carrier. He took the box hesitantly, looked inside and thanked me; but I could see the gift had troubled him, his smile was absent.

Without making eye contact, he said, 'Sit yourself down while I put these on a plate for us.' He hurried from the room. When he returned with a tray laden with cakes and tea he seemed to have recovered. We exchanged a bit of chit chat which led to the cigar box.

'I haven't seen a cigar box in a while my dear.'

'Ah, well, I've kept this box from my childhood. It's had a lot of uses over the years. It just happened to be on hand this morning when I was ready to go.'

Mr Herbert opened his mouth to speak but the words didn't come. He sighed and cleared his throat.

'Seeing the box brought back a memory I have not thought of since I was quite young. My mama kept a cigar box under her bed. I used to watch her when she took it out and lovingly sifted through its contents. She didn't know I was looking of course; it was a very private affair she had with her box. I would watch her languorous movements as she went through her ritual of opening the box and removing each item. They always came out in the same order, and returned as they'd been found. I could not understand why the contents should make her so sad. They were just a bunch of tiny doll's clothes, or so I thought. I always wanted to rush in and hug her. It's a terrible thing for a young boy to watch his mama in such a sad state; but of course I couldn't. I wasn't allowed in her bedroom. I would be in trouble if she knew I was lurking; spying on her.

I watched this ritual for years before I understood that these were not doll's clothes at all, they were real baby clothes.

I never found out about my sister until my mother died. I was 13 at the time. I found out because it was written on her gravestone.'

Mr Herbert focussed on a distance point and recited:

Mildred Herbert (b1894 – d1930)
Dearly beloved wife of Winston Herbert
Mother of Annabelle (b1916 - d1916)
and Hugo (b1917 -)

'I don't know what happened to that box,' he said, returning his gaze to the present, 'I don't know if my father knew about it. If he did he never spoke of it to me. My sister was never mentioned. It was as if she never existed.'

There was a pause in the conversation as the tea was poured.

'I have grieved two losses', Mr Herbert said as he passed me a cup of tea, 'one for a mother I dearly loved and one for a sister I would have loved, given the chance.'

He sipped his tea and looked across at me, his smile had returned.

'Do you know my dear, I have not thought of this for, I don't know how many years. It's something I never even brought up with my Annette. It feels good to have that out in the open.'

So said, he offered me a plate, 'Cake? They look mighty delicious.'

Spring cleaning certainly does bring back memories!

Remembrance (2011) *by Ann Power (Sand blasted mirror surface)*
a response to "Mama's Box"

Salamanca Series IIIb (2009) *by Ann Power (Watercolour)*

Monica's Cupboard *by Kathy Newitt*
a response to "Salamanca Series IIIb"

- CLICK -

The key turned in the lock.
Auntie Winnie was in a mood today (Auntie Winnie was in a mood most days), and so, Monica was in the cupboard again.
But Monica, a feisty, freckly faced, curly headed little girl, was not the least bit worried because she had soon discovered when she first encountered the cupboard that this was a magic cupboard.

While Monica sat in the darkness with a smile on her face, waiting for today's surprise she heard an unusual sound … *ffrrump, ffrrump, ffrrump*
As the darkness of the cupboard melted away Monica found she was face to face with a large brown animal that had long skinny legs and big brown eyes shaded by enormous long lashes.
'I've seen one of you in my story book.' Monica exclaimed 'You're a camel!'

She stood up and stepped out the door onto a soft surface. All around was a vast expanse of sculptured sand.
The sun shone ferociously in a deep blue sky.
The camel bent its spindly front legs and knelt down before her. Monica walked along its side and climbed onto its neck. **Ooh!** Monica held

fast to the camel's woven reins as it stood giving her a seat high above the desert floor. She admired an ever changing sky as the beast loped across the sands towards a striped tent in the distance. *ffrrump, ffrrump, ffrrump*

Pinks and oranges changed to deep purple hues by the time the camel stopped at the tent. When Monica scrambled down to a cooler surface of sand a small red tassel came away from the rein into her hand. Inside the tent there was a fire warding off the chill of the cold night air.
Through the tent flap the black velvet sky sparkled with a million, gazillion stars. As Monica reached outside the tent, grasping for a star that looked close enough to touch, she heard a key turn in a lock.

- CLICK -

"I'm warning you," Auntie Winnie was grumbling, "it will be straight back to this cupboard if you misbehave."

Monica, chin to chest, hid her smile. Tassel in hand she plodded up the basement stairs, her mind already thinking of ways to annoy her aunt so she would be sent to the magic cupboard again.

In the Beginning...
by Gemma Hammond

Suspended in the brilliance
Let us bask:
Tinct fervent and glistening in
Our sunshine.

I breathe the breath of you,
Your heart beats the pulse of me.

The lines of your arms,
The contours of me
Blend.
We are within.

Tongue tips caress,
Ripples pulse
Electric.
We pour our very selves.

Pearlescent beginnings
Of some wonderous promise

Let us bask.

Suspended *by Lindsay Kyle (Mixed media on canvas)*
a response to "In the Beginnning"

Poppies – An explosion in Red *by Lindsay Kyle*
(Mixed media on layered canvas)

Remembrance Days *by Gemma Hammond*
a response to "Poppies – An Explosion in Red"

Through mobiles, landlines, waiting rooms, living rooms
The unfortunate messenger arrives
Our angel of death,
Our telegram.
To deliver the news of loved ones lost:
The Dread words.

"Deeply regret George Hammond killed by cancer"

Let the aching engulf and
Smash our hearts,

"Deeply regret Roy Clough killed by leukemia"

Blast hollow wounds where we bury our dead
In fleshy tombs

"Deeply regret Kate Trutwein killed in a car crash"

The pulsating cemetery where we house our heroes.

"Deeply regret Christina Bieliauskas killed by heart failure"

Weeping the saltwater pearls

"Deeply regret May Hammond killed by a stroke"

We pin the scarlet petals of loss to our freshly engraved cenotaph

"Deeply regret Ray Williams killed by depression"

An echo of you all will linger
In the many memories we collected
Medals of our war;

Your lost battle with life.

Enigma *by Marcia Phillpott*

Were you always there
right at the beginning
lying dormant and waiting,
waiting for a signal,
for the starter's flag to fall
to send you creeping, stealthy,
upon your lethal journey?

Or did some trauma,
some outside force
disturb your balance,
upset your equilibrium,
make you cluster, join
and break away, invading
places far away from source?

Malign, malignant, ill-wishing,
one cell, just one errant cell
is all it takes.
We know so well where this can end
but why and where was the beginning?

Churchyard in Moonlight *by Anna Phillips (Pencil on Paper)*
a response to "Enigma"

Cement Works in Moonlight *by Anna Phillips*
(Drypoint)

Triptych *by Marcia Phillpott*
a response to "Cement Works in Moonlight"

Three disparate worlds exist within one frame,
they meet, collide and overlap, but do not blend.
A pastoral world, green and pleasant,
where man must work with nature and
the seasons to maintain a balance.
Overhead, a crescent moon illuminates the
swirling wind-swept sky as the heavens dance
to a rhythm of their own.

> Centre-stage, a vast cathedral
> of industry rises, ghostly and
> faceless, its ash-grey walls
> soaring up as if to launch
> into another sphere, while the
> great organ pipe belches forth,
> — but there is no music.

We live our lives suspended, precarious,
between the certainties of earth and sky.
There are no guarantees
                              on the path we tread.

Coromandel *by William S Chapman*

On the margins of some distant sea
that surges on the shores of an
alien land, the bones of great beasts
are washed up on the shifting sands,
mingled with the wrecks of wooden ships
whose timbers rise like broken fingers
from their shingled graves.
Coral and ivory gleam in the watery
sunlight and the sound of the ocean's
turbulent roar, transmitted through
the trembling earth beneath our feet,
beats in our ears like drums.

    The blackened faces of the long-
    drowned dead
    float on our sight like orbiting stars,
    and fill
    our sightless eyes with visions
    of our half forgotten dreams.

    The quiet acceptance
    of our fate is like
    the voyage of a sail-less ship
    on a tideless and unruffled sea.

    We are touched and saddened by
    the transience of things.

Transient Memories *by Sheila Lucas (Watercolour)*
a response to "Coromandel"

Work to do *by Sheila Lucas (Watercolour)*

See This Room
by William S Chapman
a response to "Work to do"

stripped bare
of all identity;

smell this room,
the must of old damp
now dried out,
and old dust now
swept away;

overlaid with smells
of fresh paint and
new-planed wood
that cover, bind and seal
its secrets in, and hide
them from the
incurious world.

It bears no trace
of what it was,
what it saw,
what it heard.
It is wrapped
in a shroud of silence,
as tightly enmeshed
as a fly in the web
that the patient spider
endlessly spins across
the sightless window pane.

The Horned One *by Augustus Stephens*

Who knows your origin?
Who knows where you begin?
Are you the same as the goat god Pan?
I know your personality,
You embody animality,
You are the essence of a virile man.

    You are the horned one,
    The dark one,
    The wild one.
    You have the power over animals.
    Yes you're the horned one,
    The bad one,
    The mad one,
        Bring it on.

You were Herne the hunter of skill,
You helped the king to his kill,
You saved the king from a wild boar.
You died hung from a tree,
Your soul was not set free,
You lead the wild hunt, the undead horde.

They feared horns on your head,
"You're evil" 's what they said,
They called you Satan the Lord of Lies.
You just say what is true,
You hold an honest view,
You revel in pleasure and you take the prize.

The Horned One *by Marion Reid (Oil on Canvas)*
a response to "The Horned One"

Sweet Smell of Destruction *by Marion Reid*
(Acrylic on Canvas)

Demon in a Bottle *by Augustus Stephens*
a response to "Sweet Smell of Destruction"

He made a special formula
He drew a secret sign
He made a strange, extravagant gesture
He called on the divine

The sickly, stink of putrefaction
Warned him to beware
The soft, sweet smell of destruction
Filled the darkening air
First a grin manifested

And malevolently leered
His courage it was sorely tested
As the thing slowly appeared

In a bottle he caged it. It swore to obey him.
Whatever he wanted it magically got him.

   Like a fire he was blazing, he went wild,
     he went crazy
   Enjoying ev'ry minute, he took himself to
     the limit
   Living life at full throttle
   With his demon in a bottle.

He asked the thing to give him money
To make him a millionaire
He gave a laugh, he thought it funny
As bank notes filled the air.

A car, a yacht, a house in the country
He asked and he got his way
Parties, drugs and women aplenty
All sex and holidays.

In a bottle he'd caged it. It'd sworn to obey
   him.
Whatever it wanted it never told him.

   Like a fire...

The demon schemed for its freedom
It knew that nothing lasts
It made him trip he fell down hard
The bottle shattered into shards.

The demon loose was fully potent
Magnificent and proud
It gloated over him for a moment
Then grabbed him and dragged him down

Down into the pit of demons and devils
There's no returning, he's still down there
   burning

In a fire he is blazing, he is mad he is crazy
Suffering ev'ry minute, his pain has no limit
His life gone replaced with sorrow
By his demon in a bottle.

Two Faced
by Hazel Bowden

The face I have,
The one you see.
The other face,
They both are me.
One is open,
And one is closed.
The first behaves
As it's supposed.
The second face;
The private me,
So very few
Will ever see.
I'm confident.
Out loud I shout.
But quietly,
I'm full of doubt.
I take life's knocks.
My smile is wide.
My hurt and pain,
I always hide.
And do I care?
You may think not.
You'd be surprised;
I care a lot.

Smile Please! *by Joan Green (Woodcut)*
a response to "Two Faced"

Raku Fired Form *by Joan Green (Raku Fired Ceramic)*

My Raku *by Hazel Bowden*
a response to "Raku Fired Form"

I want to take you out and view you in the
    morning light,
Or hold you in the air and watch your form
    absorb the night.
To take you to the fire that gave you life
    and watch you glow,
Or sparkle in the rain, as showers down
    your contours flow.
Your colour fascination binds me like the
    glaze you wear.
Come with me to the sunset, bathe your
    lustre in its glare.
Let playful sparks of copper, evenings
    fading glow ignite.
In all your many foibles, your uniqueness I
    delight.
In you I see the force that birthed you from
    the fires of hell.
Your struggles won, but deep the scars,
    and yet, they clothe you well.
A maelstrom of creation, contradiction,
    uncontrolled.
I trawled your very essence, and I caught a
    glimpse of gold.

opera tickets (bluster in a hurricane)
by Scott Baker

in silence falls softly snow as in milk as in kindness
follow angels to the field for the ten thousand
anarchies have been heralded to the dawn. short and
past and farther than the mind of a one and true love
homeliness. dance these horizons of all their worst
storms; let the auguries plough in voluptuous
monuments to the fleeting hour and the second
denomination through all streets – everywhere is there
music and it is being played. a song is every mouth
is every hall is every pontoon game shuddering in our
doorway. every child turned bad is a child turned
bad. the urge is the knowing and the life is the debt.
life itself is one inscrutable nothingness, preferred in
back alleys as the mausoleum to the lowliest bruise,
splintered about with its containment to the
destruction here made unto art by a rope bridge
swinging with white men. the urge is to go quicker
faster harder longer, and the urge is the folly of a
teen. know your numbers, high generals. i have a
feeling we are going to blast.
then down must our curtain
come –
this slum
in one
become

Dark Moods *by Winifred Wilmot (Acrylic on Canvas)*
a response to "opera tickets"

Flash *by Winifred Wilmot (Oil on canvas)*

flash *by Scott Baker*
a response to "Flash"

condemned as we are to an inner life
as though held between lines in a manuscript
at once written by time's acid pen
and recounted at the rate of the living
and by only that life
which would be endless
if it was not forced to make so much of so little

and what have i to remember?
and what leave without farewell to the silence?
as he slumped over his desk
and his astral body parted and stepped away
i go out into the hall
demolished in a loving man's mouthful
for the few firing synapses of his face in my
    mind

i walk quickly from days, dark days
dark and short like the days
tearing at the end of my jacket
days so crumpled and deformed
they are ended
before they've even began

and the smoke clears
and yellow roses drift like snowflakes into the
    trench
and the dead trees whisper: do not let me alone
and whose voices toil and rage as i open my
    suitcase
and the little black book they played choke in

writing dogma in his book
the shy beetle in the corner writes in his book
cries out from his corner and writes in his book

i have heard the siren song
i have seen the eyes of the white dogs
i have held those delicate fingers
that fly at dawn through jasmine fields
to brown and wither in a land of shattered
    bones
i have tasted desolation

so go, fall on phantoms
no noise
and be done.

Clouds *by Glyn Essex*

These are the clouds
I love to see –
giant islands,
promontories,
fat-fingered peninsulas,
whole continents
with oddly familiar coastlines –
better by far than a cloudless sky
and the fish-eyed stare
of infinity.

Cloud Gazer *by Laurence G Tilley (Ceramic)*
a response to "Clouds"

Exile Cup *by Laurence G Tilley (Ceramic)*

Diaspora *by Glyn Essex*
a response to "Exile Cup"

Out on the edge
looking in
precariously
bags packed
ready to go
so often since
God knows when

sure enough
the old blood-libel
surfaces again
threats circle
like sharks
and you're on your way to
God knows where

Fossil History *by Nicholas Marsh*

"Wha' ya gonna teach 'em today, hag?" shouted Big Man. "None of that Old Times – it's no good teaching 'em that! Show 'em joining up rain-stop – it's gonna be coming winter soon." He tutted and returned to his pile of metal as the old woman's class started to emerge from the mounds of landfill.

The sight of her charges brought conflicting emotions; their eyes were bright, but their dirty, malnourished bodies were pitiful. Their clothing was threadbare now that replacements were so hard to find. Worst of all was the lack of footwear; it was a wonder they survived at all with such cut and infected feet. Their grandparents would have been shocked beyond belief.

She was desperate to teach them more Old Times. But how do you explain computers to people who wear shards of circuit board for jewellery? How do you reference dates to those who measure their lives in summers? How do you describe motorised transport to those who think tyres are the remains of some mythical beast? Would anyone remember the fuel crisis of the early 2020s? Let alone the world that went before.

Big Man was right; today she would teach them how to join plastic sheeting.

The Rain-stop Diptych *by Carol Wheeler (Mixed Media)*
a response to "Fossil History"

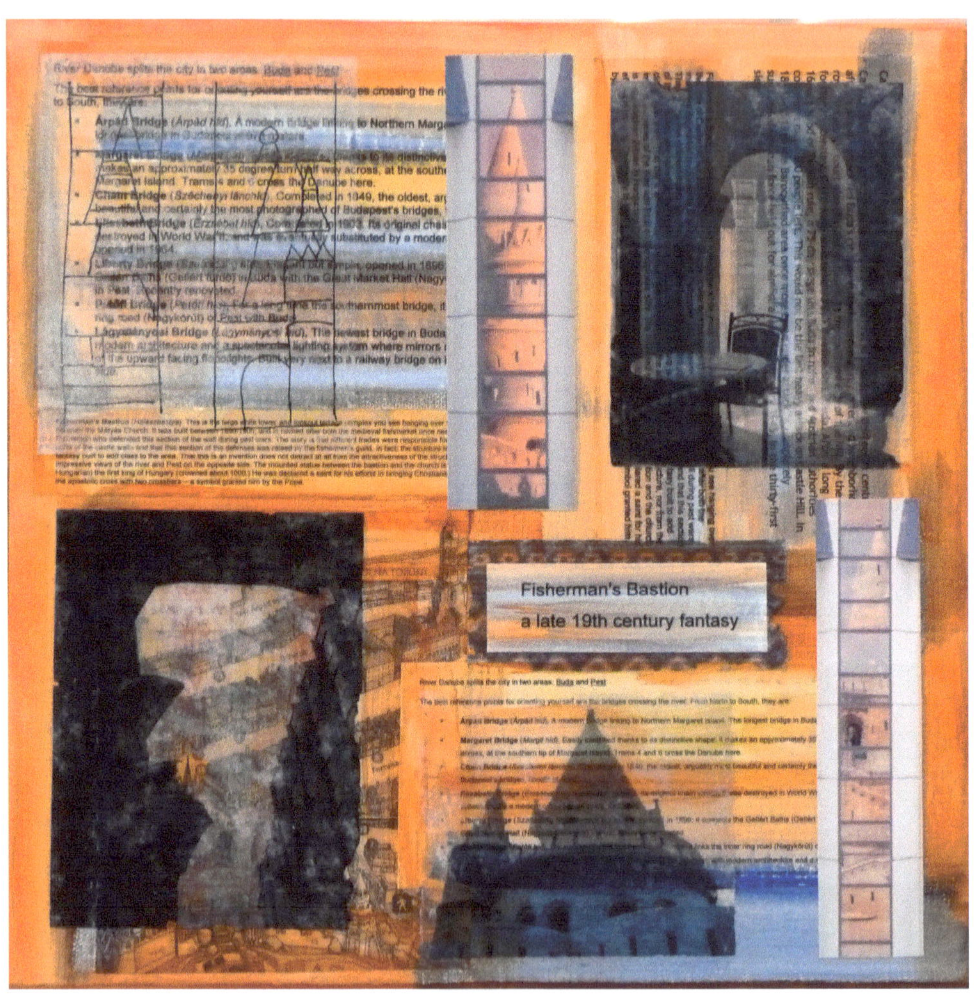

Hungarian Fantasy *by Carol Wheeler (Mixed Media)*

Return to the Fishermen's Bastion
by Nicholas Marsh
a response to "Hungarian Fantasy"

Erzsébet tucked her chin into the collars of her coat. The late autumn air stung her face, but the coat protected her, covering all but the tapping of her footsteps. The sound echoed around as if relaying her approach. *'Never catch a stranger's eye. Always be heading somewhere. Never ask questions.'* Csaba had asked questions and Csaba had disappeared. She hoped he was in prison.

From the parapet she gazed across the Danube, to Pest and the eastern plains beyond. A young couple were lingering, the man's smoky breath billowing in the still air. Erzsébet waited to take her place in the magical tower.

Why did this folly exist; this ornate fantasy with no allegiance to any institution, past or present? She looked down on parliament, down on the bold edifices and the streets where the tanks had been, and started to laugh. A small chuckle at first, then an unstoppable roar, her whole body shaking as the tears rolled down her red cheeks.

Damage *by Debbie Hibberd*

The first stuns me.
No breath, movement stilled
mouth opens then closes.
No sound but a faint clack
as teeth hit teeth.
My brain doesn't work
Any more. Pain IS in waves.
I am watching now, waiting
For the next one
And it does come! Fast,
Sharp staccato, almost
singing. Even though I'm ready,
it's like a force. A giant inexorable
force that pushes everything
out of its way shrieking
LISTEN TO ME.
What did I do wrong?
What?
Then even though I am
skinless and shredded,
scoured raw by the power,
I cannot stop it.
Keep still! Do nothing!
Say nothing! The pain
will go. There will be
no scars, no broken
bones. Just the
memories of hurt.
Words can do damage.

Stage Set IV (Damage) *by Eric Gaskell (Acylic/Oil/collage/pins on Canvas)*
a response to "Damage"

Table in a Room *by Eric Gaskell (Linocut)*

Extra Cup *by Debbie Hibberd*
a response to "Table in a Room"

I forgot again! The extra cup!
I'll get used to it. I will learn,
it's automatic to pick it up.
But now you see it's always my turn
to set the table, cook the evening meal.
We used to share things, now that's all gone.
My future wiped out in one surreal
instant of recognition, as none
of the love in my eyes reflected
back from yours. So, how did that happen?
Should I have seen the unexpected?
Read the runes had my eyes more open?
Trouble is, I liked being a two.
Rounded, right, balanced some how complete.
Now out of kilter, and missing you.
I'm not in tune, out of key, off beat.
Then I forget, so the extra cup!
I'll get used to it. I will learn,
It's automatic to pick it up.
But now you see it's always my turn
to set the table, cook the evening meal.

Great Oaks from Little Acorns
Grow *by Lin Jennings*

Hard to believe
this tough waxy seed
shed in autumn fall
of profligate plenty,
has potential
for a 1000 years – or more
of sturdy life.
Hard to imagine.

Hard to imagine
a single oak may live
for forty generations
of human family line,
silent witness
to plagues and revolutions
into a world, changed,
beyond imagination.

Hard to calculate
the gambling odds
on small nomadic groups
of vulnerable creatures,
who fanned from Africa
on a global adventure
increase to swarming billions.
Hard to imagine.

Hard to absorb
the massed intelligence
of scientific endeavour,
that sent men, gravity – light,
to bounce upon the moon,
to send probes that passed
sun's solar boundaries
into unimaginable infinity.

Imagine *by Mo Enright (Oil on Canvas)*
a response to "Great Oaks from Little Acorns Grow"

Waiting for Curtain Call *by Mo Enright (Oil on canvas)*

I Dreamt
Behind Makeshift Curtains
by Lin Jennings
a response to "Waiting for Curtain Call"

Left alone in spellbound trance
'en pointe' I now begin to dance
accompanied by quiet notes
that gently seem to drift and float,
cobweb threads of carried sound
that echo slowly all around.

He succumbed to black swan's wiles
her enchanting beauty so beguiled
that truth from him was quite concealed
but now, at last, all is revealed
his love is strong, but cannot save
he joins me in my watery grave.

Love so true just cannot die,
as the hours of darkness fly
give way to early morning glow
a new life force begins to flow,
the spell is broken from the past
we are free to live at last.

Show over, applause rings clear
storms of clapping, deafening cheers
watchers rise from cushioned seats
stretch and shuffle their cramped feet
"encore, encore" explodes around
"a star is born, a prima found"

    I roused
    rubbed aching limbs
    tender toes
    in silver, party shoes.

Sardinian Harvest *by Debs de Vries*

Scarlet poppies line the orchard's edge
Fat, cream roses sprawl the damasked hedge.
Dry bones poke through powd'ry ashen soil.
Picking, praying, sweating, the solemn pickers toil.

Lush fruit meets flesh;
Soft
in the picker's gentle palm.
Heavy
like the breast he turned to at the dawn.
Soft pink blush stains pale gold skin -
He weighs it for a moment.
Eyes closed. Remembering.

She did not stir. Did not call out his name.
But smiled a smile like flowers
drinking rain.
He pulled the sheet to warm her, as he stood
brushed salty,tangled hair: bowed his heavy head.

His pail is full. His bucket overflows.
He steady treads the path between the rows.
And squinting in the deadly tell-tale light
He sees again their single, stolen, night.

The poppies see and close their kohl-black eyes.
Fold his single, perfect guilt in scarlet leaves.
The rose drops petals at his careworn feet.
Silent witness to the summer's heat.

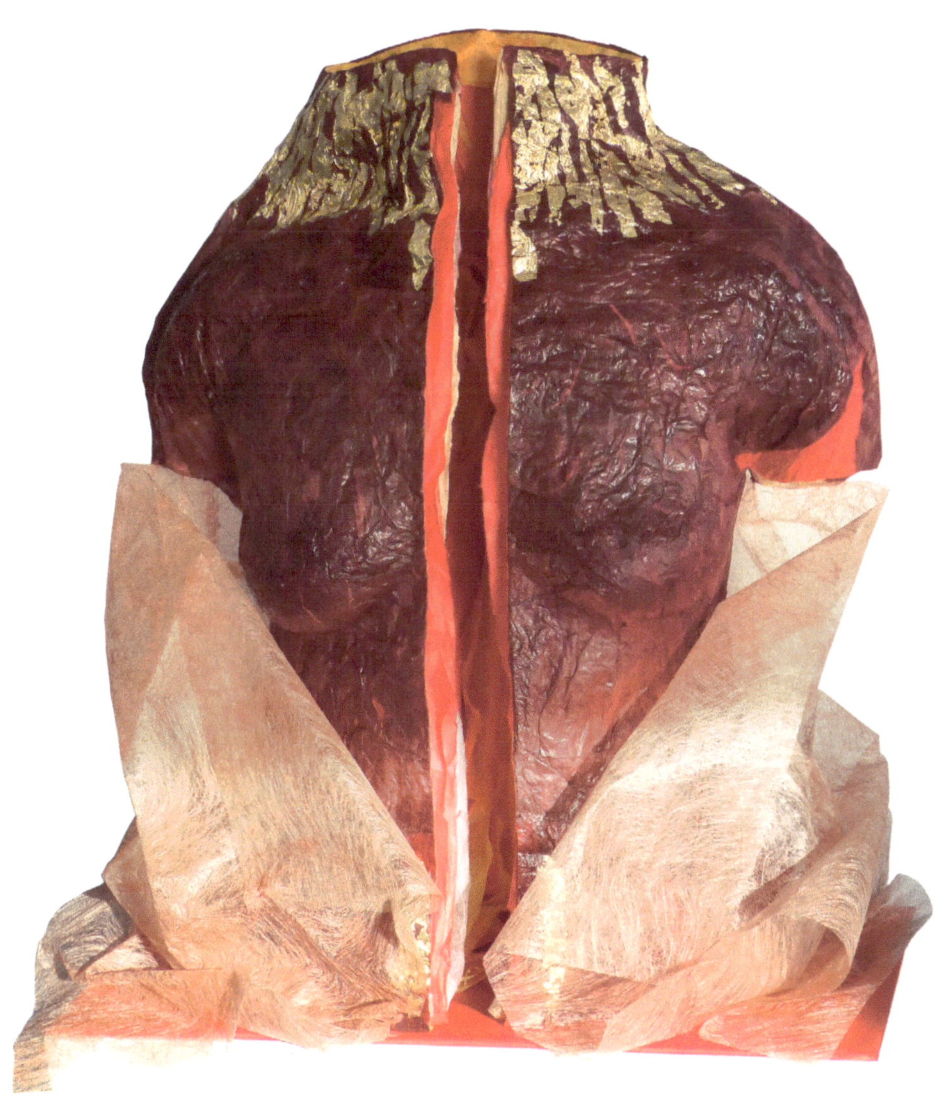

Papaule ruju *by Margarita Rubra (Paper)*
a response to "Sardinian Harvest"

Hedgerow *by Margarita Rubra (Wood/Copper/Aluminium)*

Flotsam *by Debs de Vries*
a response to "Hedgerow"

Three days.
Three days before the
gritty mist dissolved and revealed
the savaged shore.

The ocean lay mute. No sign
that she had carelessly consumed
    the beach
In a swell of passionate greed.

No matter a billion years had built it.
No matter.
It was gone.

Their pods lay
tangled in chaotic skeins of fibrous
    tube.
Life lines.
Severed. No longer pumping vital
    fluids.
Flapping like wet washing in the
soapy shallows.

Now and then a pod
the size of a horse's head
grounds on the ragged shore,
Bruised and broken.
Open like a mouth's last gasp
Exposing the soft inner spaces.
Empty.

Keening, they walk on
in a rigid line, to find one,
just one, that was emerging
when the sea screamed.

A spike of light alerts them.
Sun runs down the delicate twist
    of silver.
A spine, intact, settled in a palm
    of sand.
Only a nub, a question mark, a
    query
of the start of a beautiful mind.

This sacrum was a triumph.
See: eleven precisely articulated
    limbs
Ready to sprout.
Just as planned.
A perfect design.
Only God disagreed.

A linocut *a draft for J.K.* *by Nigel Sinker*

You go to the coast and its hinterland,
behind Burton Bradstock say,
stone walls, hedges, fields with wheat
or with cows finding north and you see
those linocut lines; they had swept
through the picture and are continuing
to Portland Bill and Lyme Regis
and on through the ocean
to be followed by turtles, or
by swallows and swifts in the air.

East and west direct births,
deaths and obeisance; there is satnav.
But life is towards the warm south
and to The North. I go to Stile End
by train or car and at last on foot.
As the gap between points
in a horseshoe of hills, it is always
charged,even in snow.
When else is such sense
of journey, arrival and dread of departing?

These lines in the picture
are not the way the world is,
they are as rills
that allow a thought,
not the forces that flooded them;
when we reckon ourselves
in momentum and energy,
the way the world is
becomes our destiny.

All those oblivious ships and planes.

Floribunda *by Vivienne Garrod-Grinnell (Mixed Media)*
a response to "A Linocut"

Autumnal Joy *by Vivienne Garrod-Grinnell (Clay and Glass)*

Vivienne's Bowl *by Nigel Sinker*
a response to "Autumnal Joy"

There's a sense of displacement, a punching
above its weight, as with The Hare with Amber
Eyes or de Temple's cross-armed spirit.

Clay slopes of pale stone,blues and browns,
pricked out in may leaves, inurn
glass cullet, fired to an emerald tarn.

In some leaves are striae that my left hand
finger tips question, the right hand resolves,
nothing is grasped or made by a single side.

I love the angle of tilt that this bowl owns,
and stance, the delicate base and generous
dish. Turn it over and find the leaves feed

a Portobello. My palms are now asking
"Who will be holding this next, or who
in a hundred years time?" As for this bowl

so for this poem. Where is the arcing power
and the countervailing force's pressure?
Here is the volume, but test each word for its weight.

Abigail *by Marion Clare*

You were made to dance under stars
and run with streams. Tidal, vital, bright.
The river of your hair is an easy, natural grace.

There is a holiness in your devotion
to motherhood. Cutting swathes across the past.
In your own small way.

At three or four, sat with your Angel Delight,
You saw six policemen kick your dad's head in.
Druggy scum.

We are not sure if the hazy picture you have is real
or an impression left
by the legend and folklore these stories become.

Told, told and retold,
adding stock to the pot.
We are fostering them into living memory.

You say *music's amazing, how it brings it all back?*
I see a smoky room, children playing in the hall.
Us?

Later we will collude and corroborate
Searching for clues. Need to define
How It Was and What Went On.

If we can catch and pin the flighty details,
we will scratch them out.
Books. Songs. Poems. One day.

Maybe you will be a mid-wife, catching babies.
Maybe I will be a writer, catching stories.
The zygote is already there.

Words like blue and purple stones
turned by the tide. When I am with you
the tide is stronger, the stones fit better.

You; spacious unbroken person.
Defying stereotypes.
I love that.

Long-limbed and blonde But more beautiful.
Honest. Mindful. Funny.
Laughter loud and free of guile.

At ten or eleven, they came again.
Kicking. Shouting. Busting the door.
Burly six-foot coppers up-ending everything.

Loss has made us sisters. It made us old women
in children's bodies. It made us young women
laughing and crying at the same time.

It will be alright.
Splintered, unhinged...
it will still be alright.

In your bright kitchen there will be
tea and honey and porridge
and children shrieking like dolphins' sonar.

The scent of patchouli and cinnamon,
bits of ribbon hanging from beams,
large paintings covered in beads,
more tea and always
more talk, more music

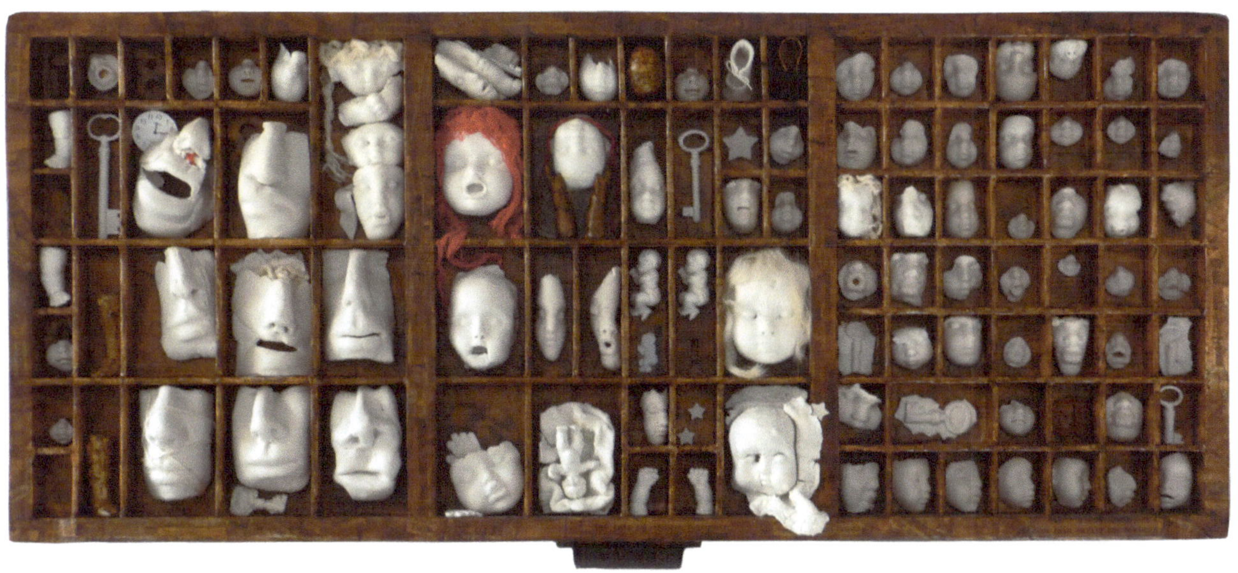

Perception of Memory and Emotion *by Judy Haslam-Jones*
(Porcelain, Wood, Collage and Mixed Media)
a response to "Abigail"

Three Temple Boxes *by Judy Haslam-Jones*
(Stoneware with high manganese glaze)

Dom Raja – A Portrait *by Marion Clare*
a response to "Three Temple Boxes"

*"The Dom Raja himself sat cross-legged on a string bed inside his
darkened room. Eight hangers on sat at his feet around a little table
on which rests a brass tumbler and half-empty bottle of clear
homemade liquor. The Dom Raja was immensely fat, nearly naked
and totally bald. His thick fingers were covered with big gold rings...I
had not brought him a handsome gift, he finally mumbled, so he saw
no reason to speak further with me."*
[G.Ward, Smithsonian Magazine, Sept 1985]

Dom Raja! Lord of the flame
Dom Raja by birth, yours is flame.
Yours are the kindling children
flicker-dart hunters. Sifters of pallid ash:
The skull, the breastbone; they are for the River
Rubies and gold; they are for the living!

Dom Raja of Varanasi, City of Light.
City of Death; constant ally,
eternal friend. O Gatekeeper, do
unlock the pilgrim soul. Dom Raja,
weave your mourners' dreams.
For yours is the sacred fire.

Survey your Kingdom Dom Raja, who is it
holding that bliss-release key?
Dom Raja! It is you...
grasp it quick, tight
in one bejewelled fist.

Dom Raja! The ascent of your star!
So dazzling, the climb. Its rise and dance
in smoking plumes.You almost own the world.
Dom Raja smiles, fire-glint eyes; Isn't this the way of life?
Isn't this the circle-shape of things?

Worm Holes *by Stephanie F. Goodacre*

No one ever told me
what it would be like.
Gardening.
On my own.

No one ever explained
how you get lost
in the minutiae
of growing things.

In another world.
All those layers
leaves, petals.
A butterfly effect.

The more I look
I notice patterns.
Mandalas; shapes
that shouldn't exist
in a random universe.

Self similarity.
The way the leaf edge
is the same as the leaf
is the shape of the tree.

Now I'm drawn
into this cauliflower
swirling in
a spiral of fractals.

And when I relax
in my own space
on my back
under that great canopy
I'm lost in worm holes

But no one at school said
become a gardener.
The possibilities
are infinite…

Wormholes *by Therése Kane (Pencil on Paper)*
a response to "Worm Holes"

Remnants – Auntie Bernadette *by Therése Kane (Pencil on Paper)*

Song for Edith *by Stephanie F. Goodacre*
a response to "Remnants – Auntie Bernadette"

a cameo
of her life
each cherished pearl
a dance
each diamond glint
a side long glance
for a glamour girl
in camisole
and ball room frock
rose water scented
long admired
yet
overlooked
left on the shelf
those faded dreams
now laid to rest
upon a satin coffer
pose a portrait
of her charms
treasured in
a song for
Edith

www.ingramcontent.com/pod-product-compliance
Lightning Source LLC
Chambersburg PA
CBHW041129100726
47911CB00002B/77